. . . for parents and teachers

What does it feel like to be different?

Sometimes it feels very good . . . such as when a child is first among her friends to learn to ride a bicycle. Sometimes it does not feel good . . . such as when a child is the only one of his friends who cannot ride a bicycle, because his legs are paralyzed. We are all like our friends in some ways, and we are all different in some ways. The things that make us alike are a part of us, and the things that make us special are very much a part of us too — often a part that is impossible to change.

Special children, like hearing-impaired Kim in *I Can't Always Hear You*, suffer from a disability. If a special child's disability keeps him or her from functioning or doing well, then it becomes a handicap. Using a hearing aid, or learning to read lips, or using sign language will help someone like Kim overcome her physical handicap.

But how can she cope with the psychological handicap that adults and children will foster in her because she is different from most of them?

I Can't Always Hear You is a good start toward breaking down some of those attitudinal barriers that we put between ourselves and disabled people. As they read about how Kim deals with being different and is accepted as a special person, children can sort out how they themselves are the same as their friends and how they differ. This will pave the way to an even better method of dealing with these issues — to actually have a "Kim" in the classroom or down the block, and learn with her.

CHRISANN SCHIRO GEIST, Ph.D.
ASSISTANT PROFESSOR OF
  PSYCHOLOGY
REHABILITATION COUNSELOR
  TRAINING PROGRAM
ILLINOIS INSTITUTE OF
  TECHNOLOGY

The author would like to acknowledge the assistance of the National Society for Deaf Children and The Royal National Institute for the Deaf.

Library of Congress Number: 79-23891

    3 4 5 6 7 8 9 0 84

Printed in the United States of America.

Library of Congress Cataloging in Publication Data

Zelonky, Joy.
    I can't always hear you.

    SUMMARY: When Kim, a hearing-impaired girl, begins going to a regular school after having been in a special one, she finds that she isn't as different as she had feared because everyone she meets has individual differences, too.
    [1. Hearing disorders — Fiction.
2. Physically handicapped — Fiction] I. Bejna, Barbara. II. Jensen, Shirlee. III. Title.
PZ7.Z398Iac   [E]   79-23891
ISBN 0-8172-1355-4 lib. bdg.

I CAN'T ALWAYS HEAR YOU

by Joy Zelonky

illustrated by Barbara Bejna and Shirlee Jensen

introduction by Chrisann Schiro Geist, Ph.D.

RAINTREE CHILDRENS BOOKS
Milwaukee • Toronto • Melbourne • London

Put your hands over your ears. Keep them there for a while. Listen.

That will give you an idea of how well I can hear. That's why I wear a hearing aid. It helps me hear better.

When I was littler, I went to a special school with kids like me. Then I started going to a regular school. Some of the kids there thought I was weird. And others laughed at me. I became afraid that I was just too *different* from other kids to ever be happy.

That first day of regular school, I was so nervous I could hardly get my hearing aid strapped on.

My mom helped me find the right classroom. Then she left to go to work.

"Hello," the teacher almost shouted. "I'm Mr. Davis. Welcome to our class."

"Hi," I said. "Um, Mr. Davis, you don't really have to talk that loud. I can't always hear you, but usually I can."

He smiled at me. The bell rang, and everyone sat down.

"This is Kim," Mr. Davis told the kids. "She's your new classmate."

Arithmetic was the first class. Mr. Davis wrote the problems on the board, and kids raised their hands if they knew the answer.

I watched for a while. Then I started raising my hand.

"Kim?"

"Eight tickery three is five," I said.

The whole class burst out laughing.

"Was that wrong?"

"Your answer was fine," said Mr. Davis. "Eight take away three is five."

"Take away," I repeated. "I can say that."

9

Mr. Davis began writing another problem on the board, but then he turned to the class.

"I wear glasses," he said. "Some of you do too. They help us see better."

I could feel my face turning red.

"Kim's ears don't work as well as ours," he went on. "She wears an aid to hear better. There are many sounds she's never heard. That can make it hard to talk. Now that I've explained, I hope you'll understand."

Even though I was embarrassed, I was kind of glad Mr. Davis had talked like that. There's nothing I hate worse than being laughed at.

A boy named Erik sat with me at lunch. He had braces on his teeth.

"What's that thing in your ear?" he asked.

"It's part of my hearing aid called the ear mold," I said. "It makes sounds louder."

"Oh, really?" said Erik. "I thought you were a robot!"

I stood up. "You should talk. You have a whole mouth full of metal!"

"It helps my teeth grow straight . . ." Erik said, but I was already running out of the room.

That night, I did my homework. Then I had a long talk with Mom while we worked on our quilt.

"I'm the only one in the world with a hearing aid," I kept saying. "And everyone treats me differently because of it."

"Every person has something different about him or her," she kept answering. "You just all have to get used to each other, that's all."

After reading class the next day, Mr. Davis said something that I couldn't quite understand. I noticed that after he said it, some of the kids went over and got in line.

So I stood up and got in line too.

At about the same time I heard people giggling behind me, I noticed that all of the other kids in line were boys.

Then Mr. Davis said, "Are there any other boys who want to go to the washroom?"

I nearly died. Quickly I stepped back to my desk.

After school was over, I waited until all
the kids had left. Then I walked up to Mr.
Davis' desk.

"It's nothing personal," I said. "But I
won't be coming back to this school anymore."

He looked at me over his glasses. "I'm
very sorry to hear that. Do you mind if I
ask you why?"

"The kids all make fun of me. Like today when I stood in the boys' line — it was a big joke."

"Maybe you should have laughed too," he said.

"I didn't think it was funny."

"I know." He looked at his watch. "Get your things together," he said. "We have just enough time."

"Where are we going?"

"To the principal's office."

"The principal?" I cried. "But I haven't —"

He just took my hand and hurried me along.

We walked down the hall to a large office.

Mr. Davis knocked on the door. "Ms. Pinkowski?" he said. "Do you have time to talk to Kim?"

The principal looked up from her work. "Of course. Come on in, Kim."

I went in and sat down, while Mr. Davis waited out in the hall.

"I'm sorry we haven't met before this," Ms. Pinkowski said. "How do you like your new school?"

"Not much. Kids laugh at me."

"Do they laugh because they think you don't know as much as they do?"

"I don't think that's it," I said. "And anyway, I do know as much as they do. I'm best in arithmetic. I'm learning to sew, and I play soccer pretty well too."

Ms. Pinkowski turned her head to the side. "Do they laugh because you wear one of these?"

I couldn't believe it — the principal was wearing a hearing aid!

"When I went to school," she said, "some of the children had trouble accepting me too."

"Do you still have trouble?"

"Sometimes. But if you're patient and friendly, that helps a lot. Expect a lot from yourself. Soon others will too."

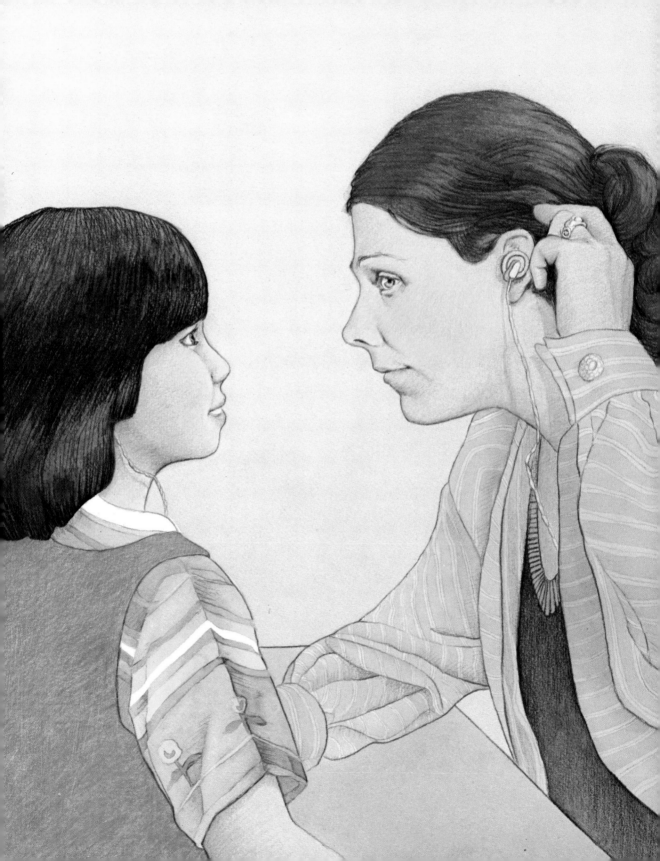

The next day, I was standing on the playground when a ball landed at my feet. I picked it up and saw Erik coming closer.

"I hope I didn't hit you," he called.

What I wanted to say was "Why? Were you trying to?" Instead I tossed the ball back to him and said, "You just missed."

He threw the ball to someone else and came over to me. "Could I look at your hearing aid?" he asked.

"Okay," I said. "But be careful."

The ear mold made a whistling noise as Erik looked it over.

He waited until I had it back in my ear before he said, "That's really neat. You know, when you first came here, I thought you were very strange. But now, well, I'm glad you're in our class."

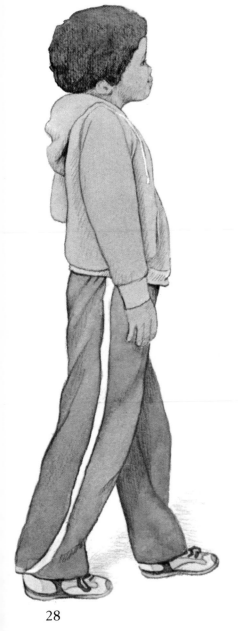

"Thanks," I said as I reached out to catch the ball. "It's hard to explain, but I guess I am kind of different. . . ."

"Not any more different than I am for wearing braces," said Erik.

"Or I am for being tall," said a girl named Sasha.

Suddenly we were surrounded by lots of kids.

"And I'm adopted," said one boy.

"And my family is the only one I know without a TV."

"I learned how to read when I was four
years old!"

"I'm a twin!"

"I get a rash if I eat chocolate!"

The bell rang.

"Race you back to the classroom!"
I shouted.

Everyone followed me across the
playground. It didn't really matter who
won. We were laughing too hard to care.